I0566012

# THE REAL PRESENCE

### BY

## DR. ROCCO LEONARD MARTINO

PUBLISHED BY

BlueNose
PRESS, INC.

PRINTED IN THE UNITED STATES OF AMERICA
PUBLISHED NOVEMBER 2019

Cover Design: Joseph A. Martino
Interior Layout Design: Joseph A. Martino


For more information on this title please contact us:
info@BlueNosePress.com

# DEDICATION

This book is dedicated to those who seek truth, find it, and have the grace and courage to follow it.

Truth is not always obvious but is always there. The assiduous searcher is sure to find it, since truth is invariable and will eventually surface as the only true reality.

# ACKNOWLEDGEMENTS

I am indebted to my wife Barbara Martino and our sons Peter and Joseph Martino who edited this book and helped me in other ways to get this book written and ready for publication. I also appreciate all the hard work done by Anne Condello who transcribed this text from my dictation.

I am also thankful to Father Robert Pesarchick, Vice President for Academic Affairs at Saint Charles of Borromeo Seminary in Philadelphia for proofreading this book and offering his suggestions for the text.

I am deeply grateful for Archbishop William E. Lori's Introduction to this book. Over dinner one night, I asked if he would do this. He did in his usual excellent fashion. Cardinal William Keeler, the former Archbishop of Baltimore, wrote the Introduction to my book "Rocket Ships and God." Archbishop Lori's Introduction to this book is a fitting twin. I am blessed to have had such long-standing friends.

Most of all I am indebted to my wife Barbara for making sure that every sentence had a subject and a verb. Also, among many other things she does for me, now drives me everywhere with great patience.

# INTRODUCTION

Recently, over dinner, when Dr. Rocco "Rocky" Martino shared with me that he would be writing yet another book, in addition to his already lengthy corpus, I was anxious to receive a copy. It did not disappoint.

In a time when so many Christians, even Catholics, do not believe in the real presence of Jesus Christ in the Eucharist, Rocky's book is a welcome apologetic. His historical-styled fiction is a real pleasure to read—both *engaging* and, at times, *playful*.

*The Real Presence* is an excellent follow-up to Rocky's earlier book, *The Resurrection*. The protagonist, Quintus, again, finds himself investigating the central Christian mysteries but, this time, it is the real presence of Jesus Christ in the Eucharist. As readers travel through history, well-known biblical figures come to life and share their own witnesses of faith in the Eucharist. Along the way, many readers will be forced to ask fundamental questions about their own faith. To be sure, Quintus' constant refrain that he is a "believer but not a follower" should cause us all to examine our consciences.

Rocky is a man of deep faith, a fact that is evident in his latest novel. As an entrepreneur, philanthropist, inventor, and even rocket scientist— Rocky has accomplished many important things in and outside of the Church and I am grateful for this most recent addition.

- ***Bishop William E. Lori,***
  ***Archbishop of Baltimore, Maryland***

November 20, 2019

# REVIEWS

There are many inexplicable mysteries in the Catholic faith; the Resurrection and the real presence of God in the consecrated bread and wine are among them. In a previous page-turner, Dr. Rocco Martino explored the Resurrection. In this work, *The Real Presence,* he explores the real presence of our Lord, Jesus, in the bread and wine consecrated at Mass. And, to make it even more interesting, he adds a touching love story. Based on the veracity of Jesus, who is clearly God, and the testimony of several eye-witnesses as well as those close to them, this book leads the reader to the clear conclusion that our Lord is, indeed, present whenever bread and wine are consecrated by those ordained to perform this miracle. It remains a mystery but one in which we can all believe.

*- Rev. Msgr. Hans A. L. Brouwers, pastor, St. Katharine of Siena parish, Wayne, PA*

Leave it to Rocco Martino to tackle another one of the great mysteries of faith that leaves you coming away with the idea that it's not a "matter of faith but a matter of fact."

In a previous book, Dr. Martino explores the death and resurrection of Jesus like a detective on a TV crime show. He uses this same device here to great effect. In this book, *The Real Presence*, with a knowledge of what everyday life was like during the days of Roman rule, Dr. Martino effectively explores the legitimacy of transubstantiation with characters who are real and relatable. He even adds a love story between the protagonist and the Pharaoh's daughter to further humanize the story.

What are the results of this search for the truth? Here's a clue - I believe!

**- *Tom Burgoyne, The Best Friend of the Phillie Phanatic and Co-Author of Pheel the Love!***

*The Real Presence* by Dr. Martino is certainly a timely read beyond being cleverly written since a recent poll said 69 percent of self-identified Catholics don't believe in the Real Presence and instead believe the bread and wine are symbols. In this novel, Quintus had proved as a Roman Tribune that Jesus rose from the dead, but he said he didn't identify himself as a Christian. Still, he was asked by Peter, and subsequently Paul, to prove the Real Presence as a Senator of Rome. Quintus became a detective of sorts, a Columbo of the 1st century to place the reader at the center of the investigation, and questioned those who symbolically represent the 69 percent of the "Doubting Thomas" of today as well as the 31 percent of the "Believing Thomas" among contemporary Catholics. There couldn't be more of a challenge or a task worth undertaking - in this novel or now. By the end of his inquiries, he too believed.

*- Kevin Callahan, Sportswriter and Author of The Black Rose, The Fish Finder, and The Chess Game*

Beginning with the final Seder meal Jesus shared with his very closest associates, Dr. Rocco Martino shares the most sacred words Jesus could have given before He was to be crucified. These are words most treasured by Dr. Martino in perhaps his most strongly expressed belief that is so basic to any Roman Catholic. Those who admire and respect the author know this may be his strongest proclamation of his faith.

Roman Catholics of the modern times, since the beginning years following the laborious writings and preachings of Catholic leaders after the Second Vatican Council, have moved forward while leaving behind the understanding and love of Jesus' Last Supper message that have been so much a part of Dr. Martino's life: "This is my body which will be given up for you." And without doubt Jesus' last words of institution of the most holy Eucharist, "Do this in memory of me" have never been forgotten by Dr. Martino.

From the mind and faith of a recognized scientist and historian, Dr. Martino has come forward with an easy and comforting read for anyone trying to understand *The Real Presence*.

**- *Rev. Milton E. Jordan, Archdiocese of Washington, DC***

*The Real Presence* is a fascinating story and a must read for anyone seeking a deeper understanding of what the Real Presence of Jesus in the Eucharist means particularly to Roman Catholics today. Especially poignant for our times is the discourse between Quintus representing the longing and searching in all of humanity, and Peter who serves as a reflection of the immense love that God has for all humans. Even the quizzical Quintus can't help but express his belief in the Real Presence of Jesus at the end of this religious novel.

*The Real Presence* by Rocky Martino is a wonderful and imaginative read for everyone!

**- *Albert W. Tegler, President & CEO, Tegler Benefits Group***

# WORKS BY ROCCO LEONARD MARTINO

## FICTION

*The Cross of Victory*

*Christianity: A Criminal Investigation...*

*The Resurrection: A Criminal Investigation...*

*9-11-11: The Tenth Anniversary Attack*

*The Plot to Cancel Christmas*

## NONFICTION

*Stairway to the Smartphone – My Life – My Invention*

*Motivational Reflections – At Sunset*

*The Coming Technology Tsunami*

*Memories: Volume I - Stories for My Grandchildren*

*Memories: Volume II - Scientist and Writer*

*Memories: Volume III - Changing the World*

*Rocket Ships and God*

*People, Machines, and Politics of the Cyber Age Creation*

*Finding the Critical Path*

*Applied Operational Planning*

*Critical Path Networks*

ROCCO LEONARD MARTINO

*Allocating and Scheduling Resources*

*Resources Management*

*Dynamic Costing*

*Project Management*

*Decision Patterns*

*Decision Tables* with Staff of MDI

*Information Management*

*Integrated Manufacturing Systems*

*Management Information Systems*

*MIS Methodology*

*Personnel Management Systems*

*IMPACT 70s* with John Gentile

# TABLE OF CONTENTS

## PREFACE

The objective of this book is an examination of the truth of the presence of God under the appearances or forms of bread and wine of the Eucharist. The mechanism chosen is to re-introduce Quintus Gaius Caesar, the major character of the book "The Resurrection," as the protagonist of this saga. The time period is the later years of the reign of Claudius (41 A.D. to 51 A.D.), perhaps about 50 A.D.

The protagonist Quintus is still Deputy Head of the Praetorian Guard. The Praetorian Guard was an elite unit scattered around the world with a mission to guard senior officials and the emperor. In some cases, it took a direct hand in removing and replacing the emperor. Such a case occurred in replacing Caligula with Claudius.

At the Seder dinner before He was crucified, towards the end of the dinner, in a very dramatic fashion, Jesus rose, took bread in his hands, broke it, and distributed to all there saying, "This is my body which will be given up for you."

Immediately after, He took the chalice, raised it up, and said, "This is my blood which is poured out for many for the forgiveness of sins." Then He distributed it to all there to drink.

1

There is no doubt that Jesus did and said this. Hence the reality of the real presence under the appearances or forms of bread and wine, depends upon the ability and power of Jesus to make these statements, and to perform afterwards.

With His many miracles, with the transfiguration on the mountaintop, with His raising people from the dead, we have more than adequate proof of the divinity of Jesus. This divinity gives Him the power and the authenticity to carry out these actions. In other words, there is more than sufficient proof that Jesus was divine.

However, a specific statement such as, "I am God" would have certainly driven home the point that Jesus had the power to convert bread and wine into His body and blood at all times. Such a statement is quoted by John at a meeting with Jesus, who said, "Before Abraham was, I am." No further proof to support His divinity is necessary.

Subsequently the plot of this novel is centered about the determination by Quintus, the main character, that Jesus' presence, body and blood, soul and divinity, is real in the consecrated bread and wine. There is no question that Jesus was divine and that He did institute the Eucharist.

Why? Christians had to experience the risen Christ and had to understand the love of Jesus for

His creatures. It was this love that led to the institution of the Eucharist, an act of pure love to provide a support mechanism. Quintus is in conflict as he begins to understand the model of Jesus in instituting the Eucharist when the mystery and power of the Resurrection is barely established. It is only after Pentecost that the nature of the Resurrection begins to be understood and accepted. The exchanges on the Road to Emmaus lead finally to understanding the Resurrection and the Eucharist with the Breaking of the Bread. The love of Jesus for His creatures in this act of love finally breaks through to provide understanding of what Jesus has done. Quintus is now able to carry out his assignment with full understanding of the full mission. A proof of the Eucharist is not the mission. That alone is insufficient. It is the acceptance of the truth of the Eucharist that is the mission. The support of this mission of Rome by Christians will lead to a solid phalanx of supporters of Rome. This support will come with some understanding of Christianity, the Resurrection, and the Eucharist. This will be a supreme act of faith based on a clear understanding of each as true miracles. Following understanding will come acceptance. Quintus does not achieve this level until he accepts what he understands. His mission, then, is to generate acceptance along with understanding of the Eucharist, the Resurrection, and the love of Christ for all humankind, especially among Christians.

# CHAPTER ONE

It was the feast of Lupercalia, the Feast of Fertility. Rome was bedecked at its most brilliant; banners, flowers, and the marching bands gave an ambience and a thrill to Rome. Each legion and the musical accompaniment paraded past the Emperor, who stood in full regalia on a reviewing stand. Next to him was an upright soldierly looking man who commanded respect from his very appearance. It was Gaius Caesar Quintus, most recently the Deputy Director of the Praetorian Guard, now being honored by the Emperor Claudius and being promoted to be a Senator of Rome. This was also the tenth anniversary of Claudius' reign. It coincided with the feast of Lupercalia and gave greater credence to Claudius as the grand Emperor of the Empire.

The general populace was somewhat mystified at who Quintus was. On the other hand, the Praetorian Guard, the other senators, and the military forces of the Empire knew very well who he was. For years, he had been the main force behind the power of the Praetorian Guard. Rumor had it he was an illegitimate son of the Emperor Tiberius. He certainly had been a favorite of the Emperor having been sent on many special projects, elite commands with special powers to different parts of the world on behalf of the Emperor.

Who was this Gaius Caesar Quintus? Rumors swirled that it was he and his sword that put an end to the Reign of Terror of the despot Caligula. Furthermore, it was he, with a cohort of the Praetorian Guard, who searched the palace to find Claudius hiding in a closet and then brought him forth. He then called out the Praetorian Guard who proclaimed him to be the Emperor of Rome. Quintus was certainly an important person and one who was at the center of the reign of Claudius. In addition, Quintus served as one of the Tribunes in the conquest of Britain by Claudius, the highlight of his reign. Claudius was certainly indebted to Quintus. Today was a major effort by Claudius in rewarding Quintus.

As the legions marched by, Claudius leaned over and whispered quietly to Quintus, "My good friend, once again thank you for your role in making me Emperor of Rome and for everything you have done to make my reign successful." Then he paused and added, "I look forward to working closely with you as a member of the Senate."

Quintus looked appreciatively at Claudius and said quietly, as it was his way, "Sire, it is my duty to do what I can to make your reign successful and to promote the interests of our Republic, Rome."

The marching of the legions continued for another hour. When it was over, Claudius, accompanied by Quintus, proceeded to the major ballroom of the palace. In a short period of time, the senators of Rome were assembled. Claudius addressed them: "Members of the Senate, it is my great pleasure to introduce the illustrious Tribune Gaius Caesar Quintus to those of you who do not already know him. He is a hero of Rome and has performed many arduous duties on behalf of the Republic. It is my great honor to propose him to be a member of this august body."

At this the entire assembly began cheering wildly. Quintus was undoubtedly a very popular figure amongst the senators of Rome. The leader of the Senate, Antonius, then rose and proceeded to the front of the assembly and addressed them. "It is my great honor to second this nomination of a great hero of Rome, and a great friend of the Senate, to be one of our members. I second the nomination of the Emperor for Gaius Caesar Quintus to be a member of the Senate of Rome!"

Antonius knew the Emperor had all the powers to do this, however he also knew the Emperor sought to improve his image with the Senate.

Once again, there was a roar of approval. After a moment or two, the Emperor once again proceeded to center front of the assembly, raised his arms, and said in a roaring voice, "I present to you Gaius Caesar Quintus, and may you all approve his election as a Senator of Rome." At which, he raised his arms and immediately it was followed by a roar of approval. And so, Quintus became not just the Tribune Quintus, but now the Tribune Senator Quintus.

The festivities continued for the entire day. Many groups of senators in turn thronged around Quintus reminiscing, congratulating him and thanking him for his many years of service to the Republic. Quite often the emperor Claudius would join the circle. It was obvious that Quintus was a favorite of the Emperor.

Not all the discussions were favorable to the Emperor. Senator Chartl sidled up to Quintus. When the Emperor was at the other side of the room, Chartl began speaking softly to Quintus.

"You must realize, Quintus, that Claudius has not had a good reign. There has been continual controversy. His expulsion of the Jews almost ten years ago was totally unnecessary and accomplished nothing but division amongst the people. This new move for him to marry his fourth wife, Agrippina, is a move that will create even more division. She has a checkered past and rumor has it that she poisoned her last husband with mushrooms."

Quintus was concerned. Chartl was certainly no favorite of Quintus. Though he did not want to create a scene, Quintus certainly did not want to spend more time listening to Chartl's gossip. In typical Senate fashion, he noticed Senator Acquimo. Quintus excused himself and went over to talk to his good friend. Acquimo immediately asked him, "What poisonous gossip is Chartl spreading now?"

Quintus laughed heartily and then continued, "He was telling me that the expulsion of the Jews by Claudius was a mistake," and without a pause continued, "He went into his fourth marriage with Agrippina, who is surrounded by rumors she had murdered her latest husband by poisoning him with mushrooms."

Acquimo gave Quintus a meaningful look and continued quietly, "You must know my good friend that where there is smoke, there is fire. Agrippina does not have a good reputation. Furthermore, she wants to see her son, Nero, as the Emperor of Rome. Our friend Claudius had best be careful when eating mushrooms presented to him by Agrippina."

Quintus spoke quietly, "A dangerous situation since I happen to know Claudius has a great liking for mushrooms." Then he paused and returning Acquimo's look added, "What do we know about Agrippina's son Nero?"

Acquimo went into deep thought before answering Quintus, "I am concerned. This Nero has a very shaded reputation for rape and murder. Nothing will stop him from achieving his goal, and that goal is to be Emperor of Rome. In my opinion, his mother will undoubtedly poison Claudius, paving the way for Nero to become Emperor."

Festivities proceeded far into the night but as it ended, each senator in turn embarked on traveling to his villa.

Quintus was the last to leave. As he did so, he was surrounded by a guard made up of members of the Praetorian Guard. They were there to escort him to his villa in the event there was any unforeseen attack by brigands who normally were present, lurking, and waiting to find a weary traveler in the night.

Quintus arrived at his villa and proceeded to the meeting room where he sat in his favorite chair for a few minutes, savoring the feeling of success that came from his election to the Senate of Rome. As he mused about the past, he remembered many of the battles that he fought and won. His thoughts went also to Princess Leah of Egypt, with whom he became enamored in the recent past, but whom he had to leave when he was suddenly transferred from Egypt to another troubled spot in the empire. As he sat there savoring his successes, he wondered about the Princess Leah and whether she would still remember him. He thought of dispatching a message to her inviting her to come to Rome. He would do that the next day.

He was troubled by the remarks of Chartl. On a brighter note, he remembered his own success in Judea. He had been sent there by the Emperor Tiberius to investigate the strange rumor of an executed carpenter who had been reputed to have risen from the dead. His investigation in Judea had led to the conclusion that the carpenter, or so he was purported to be, had actually been executed, buried, and knowledgeably dead at the time, only to have his tomb found empty three days later. It was alleged that the carpenter had been seen walking with members of his former associates in different parts of Judea.

Quintus could find no evidence to disprove the fact that he had indeed risen from the dead. If that were true, and Quintus believed it to be so, then this man was certainly a god rather than just a human. Quintus was not a follower of this sect that followed this man, a sect called Christians, but he certainly did agree that Jesus, the executed rebel, had indeed risen from the dead. Quintus sat musing about this for a few more minutes before going to bed. His last thought, as he fell asleep, was how important that empty tomb was.

A man was executed, certainly dead, and was buried; three days later the guards outside the tomb were frozen in position as the tomb slab rolled to the side and a brilliant figure in white seemed to float out of the tomb. Jesus had risen from the dead three days after his execution and was seen walking in Judea with members of his following. Quietly, Quintus shook his head. Jesus had often predicted his execution and resurrection. Quintus' investigation had proven the resurrection to be a matter of fact, not a matter of rumor or faith. Jesus was certainly a god, but that did not change the mind of Quintus with regard to his own religious preferences. On this last thought, Quintus fell asleep.

## CHAPTER TWO

The next few days were quiet. Quintus took the time to take care of his personal affairs, as well as matters requiring attention at his villa. He dispatched the message of invitation to the Princess Leah, as he did so he grinned broadly. The thought crossed his mind, "Was he finally falling in love?"

He grinned even broader at the thought.

On this happy day, as Quintus was sitting quietly in his conference room in his villa when his steward came in and said that he had a visitor, someone the steward had never seen before and a somewhat decrepit dressed individual. Quintus asked, "Who did he say he was?"

"Peter of Judea," said the steward. Quintus smiled broadly, "Of course, show him in." The steward returned shortly, followed by a tall person who looked more like a fisherman than a citizen of Rome. Quintus inwardly laughed because that's exactly what Peter was. He rose and went over to Peter and embraced him, welcoming him fondly, even though it had been years since he had seen him. He escorted Peter over to his sitting area and asked if he wanted some wine.

Peter declined. He sat quietly for a moment awaiting the question from Quintus. "Well Peter, it has been years since we last met. How can I be of service to you? By the way Peter, how have you survived the expulsion notice of Claudius?" Peter laughed as he recounted his close calls by the guards looking for Jews.

Peter sat quietly for a moment and then began speaking in a very soft voice, "Tribune, I always had the greatest respect for you, even when we were, in a sense, antagonists, during your investigation of the circumstances surrounding the mysterious disappearance of the buried body of Jesus. You were impressive with the thoroughness of your investigation. More importantly, I was very impressed with your findings that Jesus did indeed rise from the dead."

Peter paused. He seemed to be looking into space recalling memories and images from the past. Then he continued, "I have come to you to request that you engage in another investigation, perhaps even more complex."

Quintus was puzzled. Why was Peter coming to him? And what was Peter's problem? Looking at Peter with a quizzical look but remaining silent, Quintus gave Peter every opportunity to continue. Peter did.

"Tribune, if you will recall, Jesus was executed on the day before Passover. The night before is the Seder dinner. Jesus had arranged a dinner in a private room. His most intimate followers, including his mother, were present at the Seder. It was the usual dinner, with a great deal of camaraderie amongst the disciples. But towards the end of the meal, Jesus suddenly rose and stood before all of us. He took on a very serious demeanor. During the meal he had, once again, reminded us that he expected to be executed but that he would arise from the dead on the third day. He reinforced our belief when he stood very solemnly before us, took a small loaf of bread in his hands and said, 'This is my body.' Then he broke the bread and gave each of us a piece saying, in turn, once again 'This is my body.' Then he took a goblet of wine, raised it and looking towards heaven, said 'This is my blood.' Then he came to each of us with the goblet and gave it to us to drink repeating, 'This is my blood.'"

Peter stopped for a moment looking at Quintus whom was obviously very deep in thought. Then he continued. "Quintus, Jesus gave us his body and his blood and wanted us to repeat that forever after. This we do in our prayer gatherings, which we refer to as 'the breaking of the bread.' You have attended one with me in the home of some of our believers when you were involved in your investigation of Jesus' resurrection." Peter stopped and looked quizzically at Quintus.

Quintus had been very quiet, following every word of Peter, and when Peter paused, Quintus said, "Yes, Peter, I do very well remember. I am not a believer, as you know, but I have great respect for your beliefs and your people. I can see that you are troubled about something. How can I be of help?"

With an expression of hope on his face, Peter replied, "Tribune, my people have often been the scapegoats of repression, expulsion, and often execution. Tribune, my people are not understood. Perhaps one of the problems is we tend to keep to ourselves. Jews maintain their customs and rigid rules which regulate what they eat, when they eat it, and how often. There is no doubt in my mind that the behavior of my people in that fashion keeps them segregated from whatever host country they are in. Any host country would expect that visitors and immigrants would become assimilated into the nation itself and would not continue to segregate themselves from the population."

Peter stopped, and looking questioningly at Quintus, added, "Do you not find that so, Tribune?"

Quintus was somewhat surprised at Peter's honesty and perception in discussing his race. "Peter," Quintus said quietly, "I am surprised but gratified at your perception and honesty concerning the Jewish race. I have found the same characterization to be annoying and questionable with regard to their dedication to being good citizens of Rome."

Before he could continue, Peter raised his hand. Noticing this, Quintus stopped. Peter took up the conversation, "You would notice the Christians are not like that. While they may be Jews, as Christians, they behave differently. Jesus said, 'Do not think that I have come to abolish the law, or the prophets. I have come not to abolish but to fulfill it.' But what the Jews practiced in the past would be no longer applicable as the followers of Christ. Hence, Christians could remain citizens without adhering to the former customs that separated the Jewish community of their host country, in this case Rome. These Jewish customs created a barrier between Roman citizens and Gentiles. Therefore, the change."

"Becoming a Christian creates a new opportunity for Jews, as such, to become assimilated as citizens of Rome. By the way, Tribune, you know that our good friend Paul is a citizen of Rome. A long time ago, he understood that when someone professes differences in customs and in laws, they would be feared. So even as a good Jew, he has adopted the ways of Rome. As a Christian, he believes as we do, that Jesus came to change the law, not abolish it. The mitzvah did not have to be followed by a Gentile to be Christian. At our counsel in Jerusalem, Paul urged that the Gentiles who became Christians would not have to be circumcised. And so, Gentiles are welcome to become Christians without having to become Jews as well."

With an expression of hope on his face, Peter continued, "Tribune, many of our followers believe that the bread and wine during our gatherings are indeed the body and blood of Jesus, and hence of God, however some do not. I have come to you today in the hope that you can investigate this for us, not with regard to the acceptance by our followers that is true of what Jesus said is true, because Jesus said it. We his special followers or apostles, saw and heard him. We know it is true. But others who were not there and did not know him as intimately as we do can question our veracity, our witness is our support, and have other interpretations of his final comments, 'Do this in memory of me.' Jesus could speak no evil, no lie, and no dissemination. If Jesus said this is my body, it was his body. If Jesus said this is my blood, it was his blood. The bread and wine are changed into the body and blood of Jesus. I believe that. Most of our people believe that. Some do not. We would be deeply appreciative if somehow you could investigate this mystery amongst our people coming up with any ancillary support of our belief. We do not need any support with the idea that Jesus did say that, and that he could do that. Jesus was God."

Quintus remained silent and thoughtful for some time. Then he looked up and looked Peter directly in the eye and said: "I am honored that you would come to me for this request, but Peter I remain mystified as to why you came to me, and how you would expect me to find evidence that would help your people to accept these words of Jesus. I am not a believer as you know, and I am not a follower of your traditions, but I can tell you that I would accept the fact that if Jesus said this is my body, it is and was his body. If I can do that, and I am not a believer, I cannot understand why some of your believers would not accept that."

"That's exactly the point, Tribune. We can't understand why some do not believe and accept this. Some think it is merely a symbolic remembrance of Jesus. Others believe it is indeed the body and blood of Jesus Christ, and hence of God. I too am mystified as to why any of our followers would question the validity of that concept."

Both remained silent for a few minutes – Peter in the expectation and hope that Quintus would agree to this investigation and Quintus in deep wonderment as to why Peter had chosen him, and how he might even go about it if he decided to do it.

"Peter," said Quintus, "What more can you tell me? Most especially, why do you look to me to help you solve this need?"

Peter smiled: "Tribune, I was with Jesus for many months. I saw him raise people from the dead, I saw him cure blind people, even paraplegics. If that wasn't enough, together with James and John, Jesus beckoned us to follow. We climbed a high hill until we came to the top. Jesus beckoned us to stop. He went forward. Suddenly he was enveloped in a bright light and he was transformed. He became bright as the sun. His clothing and his visage took on an unbelievable brightness. Shortly thereafter he was joined by Moses and Elijah, and the three of them were conversing. I went over to them and offered to erect three tents for them on the mountain. Jesus smiled and said nothing. Suddenly from the clouds a booming voice said, 'This is my beloved Son in whom I am well pleased.'"

"And so, you see Tribune, I have tremendous proof that Jesus was God."

Peter paused. After a short period of time, he began again. "Tribune, you too have seen adequate proof that Jesus was God. You talked to many like myself who saw him die, buried, and I spoke to him three days later. And so, Tribune, that was the dilemma that Tiberius posed for you. You solved a great dilemma for the Emperor Tiberius. You proved that Jesus did rise from the dead. You made it a matter of fact. Now, I hope you can find the facts that would help our skeptical Christian followers accept that the body and blood of Christ is present under the appearance of bread and wine. I would hope that you will do this Quintus. If you do, it would be of great service to the Christians. On the other hand, I have a private hope. It is that this would be the final push that would put you into the category of being a Christian yourself. I would certainly wish that I could welcome you to our faith."

Both men remained silent for a few minutes. Quintus was very deep in thought and then rose, followed by Peter, and went over to Peter and put his hands on his shoulders. "My friend, I appreciate the faith which you have of my ability to be of assistance to you. If this can be of assistance to the Christians, then I know it would be of assistance and of value to Rome. The Christians are now the bulwark of Rome, providing a solid group of peaceful citizens supporting the government of Rome. Since so many are also Jews, Claudius may well recant his expulsion order shortly. He told me as much on the reviewing platform." Quintus paused in deep thought and then added: "I would be honored to work on this, but I want to think about it. Can you come back in two or three days and I will be ready with my answer?"

Peter and Quintus then engaged in a spirited conversation concerning the growth of Jesus' followers.

"How did you maintain remembrance of Jesus originally in Jerusalem and now in Rome?" asked Quintus. Peter thought for a moment and then began: "We did this in numerous ways. The most important, of course, was our continuing relationship, and the manner of that relationship always centered on love, which permeated all the followers of Jesus. Central to all of this, of course, was our meetings where we had the breaking of the bread. We had no real name for this process although we came to start calling it 'ite misa est', which means the end of the meeting. That was the phrase that we would use to tell all those who were praying with us that the meeting was over. Many have now shortened this to 'misa.' In my opinion, there is a great possibility that this service may be called the 'misa' to simplify it even more."

Peter chuckled. "You know Jesus pretty well set it up," he said. "Jesus repeatedly said, 'I did not come to condemn the law, I came to fulfill it.' As you know our first Christians were Jews. Hence, we adopted the ritual from the Sabbath. Since our Lord and Savior rose from the dead on the first day of the week, we established that we would have the ceremony of the breaking of the bread on the first day of the week. We also took the structure of the Sabbath. It begins with a greeting and opening prayer of remorse for sins. It then goes on to greetings. We follow that. Then we came to the point of the consecration, the changing of the bread and wine into the body and blood of our lord Jesus Christ. This followed after the readings. We then had the ceremony when each of the attendees free from sin would come to share in the bread and wine, or the body and blood of Jesus Christ. Then we would end the ceremony. We also had a remembrance of various segments and people in remembrance prayers."

"And how did you conduct these meetings?" asked Quintus.

"We would announce that we were going to have a meeting with the breaking of the bread at someone's home at a certain time. In Jerusalem, it would be one of the apostles or one of those who were ordained by us with the placing of the hands upon them. Here in Rome, until Paul arrived, I was alone. Periodically, I would find an associate or a Christian who seemed particularly exemplary in a prayer service and I would lay hands upon him and make him capable of breaking the bread and forgiving the sins of those who came to him. We came to refer to this as ordination."

Peter continued, "When Paul came, he became a great help. I had ordained Paul when he visited me after his conversion. He is a trained Pharisee and rabbi, having attended the school of the great rabbi Hillel. Paul required very little instruction from me. Most of it consisted of him asking questions about our Savior. Paul never met Jesus, except through the indirect spiritual encounters he had; first when riding his horse to Damascus, and then periodically throughout his life. Paul had a very close association with Christ even though they never met."

"But to continue, you asked about the process under which we conducted our service. We would gather and we would pray until everyone was there and then we would pray together as a group. Then we would read from the Scriptures, and this reading would be shared by one or more of those in attendance, as well as, the conductor of the service. Initially, in Rome, that was Paul or myself until, as I mentioned, I selected certain devout followers of Christ who could be ordained so they in turn would be able to conduct the services of the breaking of the bread."

"Then we would come to the consecration. We would repeat the words of Jesus, which he first spoke at our supper together for the last time on the first day of Passover prior to his execution. These words are two groups in number, at first associated with the consecration of the bread into the body of Jesus Christ. This statement is as follows, "Take this, all of you, and eat it; this is my body which will be given up for you."

"The second group that is associated with the consecration of the wine into the blood of Jesus Christ. These words are: "Take this all of you, and drink from it: this is the cup of my blood, the blood of the new and everlasting covenant. It will be shed for you and for all men so that sins may be forgiven. Do this in memory of me."

"With these words, the bread and wine have been converted into the body and blood of Christ. These are now distributed to the participants in our service who consider themselves worthy of such receipt. It is understood that no one would approach the table of the Lord in the condition of serious sin. Such are permitted the ability to seek forgiveness of their sins provided they are duly repentant. This procedure of forgiveness is usually performed before the service of the breaking of the bread. This would then permit those who come forth in full repentance to receive the body and blood of Christ during the service."

"Following the consecration, we would have prayers and remembrance on behalf of various people, including those who are departed or ill. Following that, we would say the '*Our Father*' and any other prayers that we can think of. Then we would have the distribution of the body and blood of Christ to those who wish to receive him. Lastly is a final prayer after the communion service. Then following this, the conductor of the service would say 'ite misa est' to indicate that the prayer service is over."

"Afterwards, the attendants would perhaps meet or talk for a few moments before leaving. This would constitute our remembrance service on behalf of our Savior.

"This is remarkable, Peter," said Quintus. "I find this whole effort of the remembrance of Jesus to be significant. I never met him, but I did study his resurrection and developed proof that it naturally occurred. Anyone who can rise from the dead is certainly of a divine nature. I find myself separated from a full following of that religious belief, even though I do believe it. I do believe Jesus rose from the dead. I do believe that he was divine. But I have not labeled myself, or considered myself, to be a follower of Jesus Christ because as a Roman, I have gods that I follow and that I have been satisfied with through my life. This is not to say that the day may not come when I may suddenly be converted and become a follower of Jesus Christ. In the meantime, I may be considered a believer, but I should not be considered a follower."

With a great sigh Peter said, "Quintus, you are a greater Christian than many Christians I know. I will respect your opinion that while you are a believer, you should not be considered a follower at this time."

With an upbeat note in his voice Peter asked Quintus, "Is there anything else you want me to tell you about our religion?"

Quintus smiled and said, "I think I know the answer, but Peter, tell me how you have organized the structure of your religion? Who is the head of your religion, so to speak?"

Peter laughed. "Apparently I am," he said. "Jesus put his hands upon me before he left us and said to me and to all the others, "Thou art Peter and upon this rock I will build my church."

"We took that statement to be my appointment as the head of his church. I have taken on such responsibilities and it is in that responsibility that I have come to you in terms of asking for your help. How do I handle those who claim to be Christians, but do not believe that the conversion and consecration of the bread and wine

27

turn into the body and blood of Jesus Christ? I went to Paul, who is in Rome at this time as you know, and I asked his opinion. Perhaps it would be a good idea if we three could meet in the near future. Such a conversation would certainly be stimulating."

Quintus smiled and threw his hands up. "It would be great to see him again. He impressed me as a brilliant and dedicated man. He certainly is devoted to whatever he believes as he had me convinced when I met with him in Tarsus before he had his conversion. Even then, there seemed to be some notes of appreciation of Jesus, even though at the time he was condemning all such followers of Jesus. I find it ironic that Paul is now one of the most dedicated Christians in your group." Quintus smiled even more proudly. "Peter, bring him with you. It will be a great conversation."

And with that, the meeting came to an end. They arranged to meet in a few days with the promise Peter would bring Paul to the meeting. Quintus summoned his steward to take Peter to the door.

Peter grasped the hands of Quintus and looked directly at him. "My friend, I thank you for your consideration. I will return in a few days with Paul to see what your reply is to my request. No matter what it is, I will always to my last breath have nothing but the deepest respect for you." Peter then bowed and awaited the arrival of the steward.

## CHAPTER THREE

Why should Quintus help them? Peter pondered the question deeply. The answer fortified his belief that Quintus would help. By helping them, he helped Rome.

It was two days after the Sabbath when Peter and Paul came to the residence of the Tribune Quintus. Upon the steward escorting them into the presence of Quintus, Quintus showed a great deal of happiness in greeting Paul.

"Paul, I still remember the day in Tarsus when we had our conversation about Jesus before my investigation of his resurrection even began. At that time, Jesus was known to me only as a good man. I knew you were condemning the followers of Jesus, so I was somewhat surprised when, during our conversation, you admitted that Jesus was a good man and you sometimes wondered how a good man, as such, could be condemned by so many. Then you had your conversion and became one of the leading exponents of the creed, if we can call it that, of Jesus Christ."

"You must know that I, in turn, have become a great believer in the divinity of Jesus Christ, and most certainly that he did rise from the dead. My examination of that phenomena made it a matter of

31

fact; not just a matter of faith amongst believers. With that Paul, I welcome you to my home and I welcome you with your companion Peter, of whom I have a great deal of liking and respect. I expect that this afternoon we will have a very spirited and interesting discussion about the real presence of Jesus Christ in the bread and wine that you have at your meetings, which are unnamed, except for the appellation used to terminate them 'ite misa est'."

Paul grinned proudly. "Tribune, thank you for such a gracious welcome to your home. Congratulations again on becoming a senator of this great republic. It is men like you who will lead this nation to greatness in all of Rome's history. It is my hope that your nation will also become a solid partner of the followers of Christ, commonly known as Christians. It is my hope that Rome will not only be a supporter of the Christians but will become the bastion of support for this group of people."

"That is why I am here. I firmly believe that that will be so and during my lifetime; I hope to play a significant part. And so, Tribune, how can I be of assistance to you? Peter has told me that he has asked you to lead an investigation and to establish any reality of the conversion of bread and wine into the body and blood of our Savior, as he did, and as we do. There are some, of course, who look upon this phenomena, and perhaps even benefit from it, but still have doubt and disbelief, beyond a tingling of such disbelief to a strong disbelief. It is our hope, Peter and I, that your investigation will find a way to make this a matter of fact and not a matter of faith, just as your study made the resurrection a matter of fact and not just a matter of faith."

Quintus was silent. He looked quizzically at Peter and at Paul. He continued to remain silent. Then abruptly, he seemed to shrug before addressing Peter and Paul, with his eyes moving back and forth between the two men.

"Gentlemen, you give me great credit and I thank you for the great compliments." Quintus stopped and remained lost in thought for a few moments before continuing. "I know what your objective is. As to how I can do it has yet to be determined. Give me a few days and please come and visit me again. We will discuss the how. For now, that how must remain a subject of deep thought."

Quintus remained silent for a few moments, alternately looking at each man in turn. Finally, he began again: "I have no doubt as to the importance of this assignment, and as to its difficulty. I must admit, at this time, that I am not convinced that I can do it, or that I want to do it. I would like to hear from each of you as to why you want me to consider undertaking this study. I know it will be of great importance and is of great importance to your people. But can it be done? And also, am I the right man to do it? Granted, I did succeed in my study of the resurrection of Jesus; I concluded that it did occur, and that Jesus was divine. But gentlemen, remember, I am not a Christian. I have strong convictions that what you espouse is correct, but it has not induced me to become a Christian, even though I believe that you are, in truth, linked to a divine nature. There is a great deal of difference between respect and conviction on one hand and union in terms of the sect beliefs on the other."

Quintus remained silent for a short period, then looked directly at Peter. "Peter, as the head of your church, you have come to me and asked me to undertake this study. Why? Why me? Do you even need this study? Granted that you have some members of your sect questioning the validity of this concept, but why is that important?"

Quintus once again stopped. After a moment, he looked directly at Peter and continued, "Well, Peter, tell me what you think."

Peter remained silent momentarily, looking directly at Quintus. He darted a glance at Paul and seemed to get an approbation from him. Then he turned to Quintus. "Quintus, we think you are the perfect man to undertake this assignment. We know that you will pursue it with diligence and arrive at conclusions that are based on solid findings. We may not agree with your findings. We think we will, but we cannot at this time say for sure that we will until we hear what your recommendations and findings are. We have no doubt whatsoever of your ability to undertake this study, nor do we have any reservations as to where your study may lead us. In fact, we are convinced that this study completed by you, a non-believer, and a man of impeccable credentials and reputation, will have a profound impact upon our followers. That is why we come to you. You are a person of integrity and you are a person whom we are sure will study this problem in detail and arrive at a solution, and if not, recommendations that will be acceptable to our people. We hope that the conclusion that you come to is the one that we believe to be so. That is, that Jesus did institute the priesthood whereby we have been given the power to change bread and wine into the body and blood of Christ."

Peter paused for a short period and then added, "That is our belief." Then looking directly at Paul said, "Paul, do you have anything to add?"

In his usual energetic demeanor, Paul smiled broadly. "Peter, you have said it all. You were there at the supper on the first night of Passover. I was not. As a matter of fact, as you both know, I never met Jesus. I did indirectly, of course, when he pitched me off my horse and made me see the light of day." Paul laughed for a moment and then continued: "Why do so many of our followers not believe this to be so? Why do so many believe this solely to be a ritual in remembrance of Jesus?

"What do we need to do to reinforce this belief so our followers will accept the truth that Jesus did change bread and wine into his body and blood; and that he gave us, his apostles, the authority to continue this memorial of Him?"

"There is no doubt in my mind that we need a study and an examination of this and especially if it is conducted by someone like you, Quintus." Looking directly at Quintus, Paul continued: "And so I agree totally with Peter. I hope you will undertake this study. I firmly believe that you will have significant influence upon our followers."

Paul paused for a moment while continuing to look directly at Quintus and said, "So take whatever time you need to decide if you will take on this study for us."

## CHAPTER FOUR

Quintus pondered what he had been asked and thought very carefully of what his next step would be. But then it suddenly came upon him. Why not ask Peter and Paul if they believed in the real presence, and if so why; and if not, why? Quintus thought more on this for a moment or two, then turning to Peter asked: "Peter, do you believe in the real presence? And if so, why? And if not, why?"

Peter was stunned for a moment. He became silent as he decided how best to answer Quintus. Then Peter began with a broad grin, "Quintus, you are extremely clever, but we knew that in advance."

Peter seemed to brace himself and to lift his shoulders and to stand even more erect. "Quintus, you must realize we were with Jesus when He did this, when He made these statements, at our last dinner together. There is no doubt in my mind that what He said is absolutely true. He gave us the ability and the authority to change bread and wine into His body and blood. That is my belief. That is the belief of all those who we have anointed to continue this tradition." Looking directly at Quintus, Peter added: "Quintus, be assured, I believe totally in the real presence. There are no ifs, ands, or buts in my belief. It is complete."

With his statement concluded, Peter continued to look directly at Quintus.

Quintus turned to Paul. "Paul, you were not there at the dinner. Do you believe that you have been given the power to change bread and wine into the body and blood of Jesus?"

Paul casually looked at Quintus, glanced at Peter, and looked again directly at Quintus. In a very quiet way, he began: "Be assured Quintus, I believe strongly that I have been given the power to change bread and wine into the body and blood of Jesus. I was not at the dinner, as you say, but is not necessary for me to have been there. Just to be told by people whom I believe totally, such as Peter, James, and John, that Jesus said this, is enough for me. I believe that Jesus did change bread and wine into his body and blood, and also gave us the power to do the same. Peter gave me the power by anointing me when I visited him after being thrown from my horse." Paul chuckled. "It was a crude but effective way to get my attention." Paul grinned even broader. "It worked!"

Paul paused for a moment and then looking directly at Quintus again, added: "And so Quintus, you have heard testimonials by both Peter and me, that we have complete belief in the real presence. Such is, I hope, the same kind of statement that you will hear when you question other Christians."

Quintus asked: "Peter, why did Jesus institute this? What did he hope to accomplish by instituting the conversion of bread and wine into his body and blood by whomever is anointed to do so?"

Peter did not hesitate before answering. "Because he loved us. Jesus continually preached love, telling us to love God above all else, and our neighbors as ourselves. He in turn loved us. Because of his love, he wanted to leave us with a remembrance of himself plus, a reinforcement of his teachings. This reinforcement was vital for him. He wanted to leave us with his teachings plus the help to follow them. That is why, Tribune, he instilled the same ability for our consecrated ones to change bread and wine into his body and blood."

Quintus had listened carefully to Peter. He had much to digest. After a short silence he added: "Peter and Paul, I am gratified in your trust in me with this request and assignment. I am gratified to hear what you said, but I had no doubt whatsoever that that would be what you would say. My purpose, as you may have ascertained, in asking this question of you is not because I had doubts, but rather I wanted to hear the answer so I could compare what you said to what I expect to hear from your followers as I question them. I must, as you very well know, engage in a very detailed study of this question for my opinion and findings to be of any value to you.

This must, of course, include conversations with Christians, and with non-Christians." After a short pause, Quintus added, "The real question is why do some believe and some do not, all with the same knowledge?"

After a brief pause, Quintus continued: "And so gentlemen, you have left with a request, which I will consider very carefully, and be prepared to give you an answer in a few days' time. When I am ready with my decision, I will send for you. In the meantime, please think in terms of how you might be of assistance to me as I prepare to embark upon this program of inquiry." And with that, Quintus rose, and went over to both Peter and Paul and asked, "Is there any other matter you wish to discuss, or any other questions you may have? If not, then I believe our session here is over." Hearing nothing from both Peter and Paul, Quintus summoned his chief of household to escort Peter and Paul to the exit.

When they had left, Quintus sat quietly for several minutes. He pondered the request and went over in his mind how he would proceed if he did accept the request made by Peter. First, of course, he would have to rely on people he knew. He knew that two of his Centurions, Longinus and Cornelius, were Christians. He would have to discuss the question with them thoroughly. In addition, he would have to seek out Christians in various levels of life in Rome and elsewhere to examine the replies to his questions. Most of this would be done individually but Quintus foresaw the need for an examination in a group session. This would best be done at the conclusion of the ceremony of the breaking of the bread. For that he would have to attend such a prayer meeting and ask the leader who directed the ceremony if he, Quintus, could address the group at the conclusion of the prayer service.

Quintus was somewhat mystified at the naming of this prayer session. He was not too happy with the long phrase 'ite misa est' which represented that the ceremony was over. He would prefer to refer to this as 'misa'. And perhaps that would be the name that would be attached to this prayer service in years to come.

Now that he had the beginnings of a plan, Quintus sat for a moment. The real presence was associated with the conversion of bread and wine into the body and blood of Jesus. How could this be? Very simple, thought Quintus. If Jesus had the power to rise from the dead, converting bread and wine into his body and blood would be a simple act. With that, Quintus directed his attention to other matters of his household.

# CHAPTER FIVE

The next morning Quintus began taking care of matters that he had not completed the previous day. First, he sent word to Longinus to please come and meet with him at his convenience. Then he also sent a similar message to Cornelius. It was his intention to discuss with these two Christians, both of whom were Centurions, and both of whom were quite well known to him. Longinus in particular would be of interest. Longinus had been the Centurion in charge of the execution of Jesus of Nazareth. As the Centurion in charge of this execution, it was his duty to be sure that the criminal was dead. The normal procedure was to remove the criminal from the cross and then to throw the body down the hill to be devoured by the animals. It was cruel and senseless but so are all executions. Since Jesus had a tomb, donated by Nicodemus, his body was taken down and prepared for burial, and then placed in the tomb.

It was the duty of Longinus to be sure that Jesus was dead. As a result, he was the one who took a lance and pierced the side of Jesus until water and blood came out. Then Longinus gave the command to take Him down from the cross.

Quintus had heard that Longinus became a Christian shortly after that episode. It must have affected him greatly. Quintus was looking forward to his discussion with Longinus. As he completed these tasks, his steward came in and told him that a message had been received. Princess Leah had left Egypt and was expected to arrive at Rome in a few days. Quintus immediately set about preparing for her arrival. He instructed his steward to locate a villa for him nearby since he had determined to have Leah stay in his villa. He then instructed the steward to secure adequate staff for the villa for the comfort and convenience of the Princess. He further instructed the steward to contact the tribune, Antonius, who was in charge of the garrison of Rome and ask if a cohort of legionaries could be assigned to the security of the Princess. He further instructed the steward to arrange for a cohort to meet the barge from Egypt that would arrive shortly, and to escort Princess Leah to his villa in Rome. Then he went about his other tasks. Later in the day, the steward came in and told him that the Centurion, Longinus, was present in the arrival area of his villa. He told the steward to bring Longinus to him.

Longinus was as erect and soldierly as ever. His hair was grey, and he seemed somewhat careworn. The two old friends greeted each other. Quintus noticed that Longinus still had his short sword at his side. Quintus was somewhat surprised, but not really. Longinus had always been very soldierly and one of the better Centurions to have served under his command. Longinus had been assigned to him when Quintus served in Judea. When Quintus left, Longinus remained in Judea, and it was in that capacity that he came to be assigned the task of the execution of Jesus.

"Longinus, my friend, how are you? It has been many years since we last met. I have a matter I wish to discuss with you, but before that, tell me how you have been."

Longinus seemed to take a deep breath: "Tribune, much has happened. Some good, some difficult, and some bad. But so is life. You know I became a Christian. After the episode associated with the execution of that innocent man Jesus, I examined, in greater depth, information about the good that He did in his lifetime and I was surprised at the hatred exuded towards Him by some members of his own race. In my opinion, His execution was nothing but outright murder. But yet that was my duty and I executed it to the best of my abilities since I am a Roman soldier."

Longinus paused for a moment and seemed to brace before he began again. "Tribune, you must know that the emperor Caligula condemned me and my entire family to lions in the Colosseum."

Quintus was startled. He had heard something of that rumor that Longinus had been condemned by the Emperor Caligula, but he had found it difficult to accept that, since Longinus was one of the great heroes of Rome, and one of the best commanders ever to serve the legions.

Quintus asked Longinus: "Tell me what happened. I find it hard to believe that even a person like Caligula would stoop so low. Caligula was an animal. It was my great privilege to participate in his execution which led to the selection of Claudius as our Emperor. So, tell me Longinus, what happened?"

Longinus seemed to brace again: "Tribune, it was terrible. I was arrested, and together with my family, my wife and two young children, was placed in the holding area in the Colosseum. The next day there was a roar in the crowd and the gates were opened and we were pushed out by the guards. There were a number of other Christians who were also pushed out. I instructed my wife and my children to stand behind me and no matter what happened not to depart and not to run but to stand behind me to stay together as a solid group. Shortly after, as we huddled, there was a roar from the crowd again as the other gates opened and the lions came into the Colosseum. There were six of them. The looked ravenous. There were other Christians in the arena with us. They made the mistake of being separated. Some ran and tried to run back to the gate where we had exited. The lions immediately went for the individuals. They made short shrift of these individuals and began to gorge on them. Then one lion, not being satisfied, turned towards me. As he approached, I took my short sword which I had retained. The guards had allowed me, because of my rank, to do so.

As the lion approached, I ensured that my family was huddled behind me. As the lion made ready to pounce on me, I slapped the short sword heavily against its nose. The lion was startled. It drew back. I thought it would leap on me, but I ran towards the lion and slapped it hard on the nose again. The lion was surprised and went and found other game. Throughout all of this, I made sure my family was huddled behind me so that no lion could pick off one of them. Together with the other five lions, it soon made short shrift of the huddled and individual Christians that were also in the arena, but they stayed away from me. Having satisfied their hunger, they left. There were a few other Christians still alive, but I thank God that my family and I had survived."

Quintus paused for a moment, taken by the bravery of his former comrade, and then began, "Longinus, I knew you were a brave man. I also knew you were very clever. I think what you did in the arena not only saved your family but stands as a beacon and a symbol of what can be done to survive."

"Tribune, you know I am a Christian, and I know that Jesus rose from the dead. I believe that Jesus may have even been by my side that day. I had extra help, far beyond what I could do with my own arms and a short sword. I firmly believe that I was saved by the power of Jesus."

Quintus thought very carefully and then began: "You know that I believe that Jesus did rise from the dead, and I accept many of the beliefs of the Christians as being valid, but you know also that I have not renounced my own faith, and I am not Christian. But I do believe what you say, but even then, I know that your own bravery and strength was enough to have the lion leave you alone."

Longinus continued, "Jesus was murdered. He was executed by Caiaphas, who engineered the entire trial arrangements which were a farce. I knew what was going on but could do nothing about it. I was assigned as head of the execution squad. It was my cohort that escorted Jesus as he carried the cross. It was my men who found Simon of Cyrene to help Jesus carry the cross. Simon was an absolute gentleman. As we approached Calvary and he turned the cross over slowly to Jesus, I made it a point of thanking him for what he did."

"Had the Jewish people known that it was Jesus being crucified, I think they would have risen up and rescued him. They loved Jesus. They did not know it was him. This beaten man with a crown of thorns and his face all bludgeoned was not anyone they recognized."

Both remained silent until Quintus broke the silence with this question, "Is that why you are a Christian?"

"No," said Longinus. "I became a Christian after that fateful first day of the week when we all heard thunder in the sky and saw bolts of lightning come down on Peter's head. He spoke, and I know for a fact that Peter, at that time, did not speak Latin, but only Aramaic, but I heard Peter in my own Latin. Other members of my squad also heard him in their own native languages. That was impressive. But more impressive was what he said. He spoke of Jesus, he spoke of his resurrection from the dead, he spoke of his conquest of death. Only a God can do that. His words convinced me, and he baptized me that day. That is how I became a Christian."

"In other words," said Quintus, "I can have faith that what Jesus promised was happening."

"Yes," said Longinus. "I did not, for a moment, question the promises of Jesus."

## CHAPTER SIX

Once Longinus had completed his remarks and memories of his terrible experience in the Colosseum, Quintus began his questioning.

"Longinus, my friend, I have been asked by Peter and Paul to ask various Christians if they believe that Jesus did change bread and wine into his body and blood, and if this has continued to this day. To be very specific, do you believe that, when you attend the ceremony of the breaking of the bread, the bread does become the body of Jesus, and the wine does become His blood?"

"Tribune, yes. I do believe that there is a conversion of bread and wine into the body and blood of Jesus."

Quintus was not surprised at the answer, but he was determined to go further. Looking directly at Longinus, "Why?"

"Tribune, you know that I pierced the side of Jesus with a lance. I know he was dead. I know that we buried Him. Yet I saw Him walking in the streets in Jerusalem afterwards. Jesus conquered death. He had the power to do that. If He had that power, there is no doubt in my mind that He had the power to change the bread and wine at the dinner with his followers. I also strongly believe that He has the

51

power to continue that process even to this day, but He is no longer on earth. Jesus was human, but He was much more. He was God. There is no doubt in my mind that He was God. I am told that there are three persons in our God: God the Father, Jesus, and the Holy Spirit. How this happens to be and how it can be, is beyond my perception and understanding. But I do believe. I believe Jesus was God. I believe Jesus was the Son of God. I believe that He reigns in heaven forever. So why should I not believe that when Jesus said that he changed the bread into his body, and the wine into his blood, that it happened? And if Jesus said that this would continue and that he gave the power to those upon whom he saw fit, then, of course, I believe that when our anointed ones, at the breaking of the bread ceremony, say 'This is my body,' it is Jesus changing the bread into his body. When the anointed one says, emulating the words of Jesus, 'This is my blood,' that indeed it is the blood of Jesus."

After a short period, Longinus continued, "And so, Tribune, you understand why I believe this to be so. Why it happens, how it happens, is beyond anything that I can conceive. I just believe it happens."

Quintus remained silent for a moment. Then he grasped his friend's arm. "My friend, I believe you. I believe that you believe. I have been charged with an examination of this amongst Christians and I will proceed to complete my assignment as requested by Peter and Paul." After a short pause, Quintus continued. "Thank you for coming. If you can think of anything else that you could add to this discussion, please say so. If you can think of anyone that it would be wise to meet, please let me know."

Longinus looked at Quintus resolutely. "Tribune no, there is nothing more I can add. I think your assignment will bear much fruit. I think that just as you examine the circumstances associated with the death of Jesus, and the disappearance of his body, leading to your conclusion that He did indeed rise from the dead, I am equally certain that you will find that Jesus does continue to change bread and wine into His body and blood."

With that, Longinus saluted Quintus, and took his leave.

Upon the departure of Longinus, Quintus resumed his preparations associated with the imminent arrival of Princess Leah. The rest of the day was spent in all these details. In midafternoon, the Centurion Petronas visited him, together with a cohort of the legionaries. These had been assigned by the Tribune Antonius to be an escort and guard for the Princess Leah.

## CHAPTER SEVEN

Quintus was discussing the arrangements of his villa with his steward when word came that Cornelius had sent a message. Quintus read the message which said that Cornelius would be arriving the day after tomorrow. Cornelius planned to make himself available to meet with Quintus upon his arrival.

When Cornelius arrived, Quintus had his steward bring him to his meeting room. There he began by welcoming Cornelius for taking the time and effort to come and visit him. He then proceeded to tell Cornelius that he had been asked by Peter to examine this whole concept of the conversion of bread and wine into the body and blood of Jesus. "Cornelius, I believe you are a Christian, are you not?"

Cornelius looked directly at Quintus. "Yes, I am. I was converted by Peter when he visited me in Caesarea. And I have attended various meetings with Peter and with other Christians and what we are coming to call 'ite misa est' or the shorter version 'misa'."

Quintus smiled broadly and encouraged Cornelius to continue. "I was aware of this. I have had extensive discussion with Peter on how the ceremony and the ritual came to be established, and how the name is rapidly becoming 'misa'." Quintus paused, then looking directly at Cornelius again began, "So, tell me Cornelius, what your reaction is to all of this?"

"Very briefly, Tribune, I believe. I believe that Jesus certainly had the power to create a process whereby bread and wine are changed into His body and blood. That occurs at all occasions where we have such a conversion process by the anointed one who is directing the 'misa' service."

Cornelius paused for a moment and then began again, "I know there are some Christians who do not believe that there is an actual change, but rather that this is a symbolic representation. I do not share that belief. I believe there is an actual change. As a result, we maintain the symbolism, but we also have a real change into the body and blood, just as Jesus said it would be."

Cornelius looked down and he thought for a moment and then looked up. "I know it is difficult to accept this. It is a difficult belief. Many of Jesus' disciples parted from Him on this very point. His apostles remained. They were present at the Seder dinner before He was murdered. They were also present when He arrived and met with Him after He rose from the dead. They know personally that Jesus rose from the dead. They were present when He said for the first time at the Seder dinner, 'This is my body' and also, 'This is my blood.' How could they think otherwise?"

Quintus was not surprised at what Cornelius had said. He looked at Cornelius. "Cornelius, I can accept what you are saying, that you believe this. It becomes a question of, do I believe it. Frankly, Cornelius, I don't know. Why did Jesus do this? I too investigated the resurrection of Jesus. I did not see Him since He had disappeared before I arrived in Judea. But I do believe that He did rise from the dead. Which is startling in its own right. There is no doubt whatever in my mind that that occurred. I'm on the fence, so to speak, with regard to His real presence. But then again, He said this. And I believe that He said it since I was told by people whom I implicitly believe. Do I accept?" Here Quintus paused for a lengthy period of time. Then he continued, "I do not yet accept because I am not ready to become a Christian. But I'm very close. Give me some time, Cornelius. When next we meet, I may be able to say to you that I am a Christian. But not now."

Quintus paused again for a moment and then began, "Cornelius, you can do me a great kindness, and advance my investigation significantly. Please canvas the Christians that you know and secure their opinion as to whether they believe or not, and why not or why. Then, report back to me if it is convenient, or send the information in a papyrus. In the meantime, I will continue my investigation."

Then Quintus walked over to Cornelius and grasped him by the arm. "I appreciate your coming. Now let me exercise our hospitality to make your trip worthwhile."

Cornelius smiled broadly and with a look of admiration toward Quintus said, "Tribune, just being in your company brings back many fond memories of our times together. It is a privilege for me to be able to spend this time with you."

With that the two walked to the dining room where a sumptuous banquet had been prepared. Later that day, Cornelius took his leave and returned to his post in Umbria.

Quintus then called the commander of his guard detail to come to him. Centurion Adonis came, greeted Quintus and asked how he could be of assistance.

Quintus explained what he was doing with regard to an examination of the concept of the conversion of bread and wine into the body and blood of Jesus. "My good man, I do not know if you are a Christian or not, but I want you to undertake this study. By the way, are you a Christian?"

"No, I am not, Tribune, but I do admire them. Many of my legionaries are Christians but, I am not."

"That is no matter." said Quintus. "It might have helped, but it is not material. I want you, Centurion, to investigate this concept that Jesus said that He was establishing the process whereby bread and wine would be converted into His body and blood. Please see how many people you can meet who are Christians who will tell you whether they believe this or not. I want you to establish a total study throughout Rome. Ask as many people as you can find, that are Christians, their opinion of this point. And report back to me as soon as you think that you have exhausted your possibility of finding people to question."

"I also want you to try and find any who were present when Jesus fed 5,000 with seven loaves and two fishes. Ask them if they know what He did and if they understand the significance of this ritual. In fact, how did it relate to Jesus changing bread and wine into his body and blood?

Do you understand?"

"Yes, Tribune."

With that, Quintus dismissed the Centurion Adonis.

He then continued his preparations for ensuring that all was ready for the visit of Princess Leah. As he did so, he felt an increasing joy permeate his whole being.

# CHAPTER EIGHT

Quintus was thrilled to receive word that Princess Leah was approaching the coast of Italy at the entrance to Tiber. He immediately set about preparing for a royal welcome at the Emperor's pavilion. He had already spoken with Claudius, who was himself looking forward to greeting Princess Leah. When Claudius asked Quintus who she was, Quintus with a deep grin replied, "The daughter of Pharaoh." Claudius laughed just as Quintus did, well knowing that had Leah been a boy, she would be the next Pharaoh of Egypt.

Preparations went rapidly and soon there was a full staging at the Emperor's pavilion of a welcome suitable for a princess, in fact the crowned Princess of Egypt. There were mass bands, garlands of flowers, dancers, and a large number of legionaries in full dressed uniform awaiting the Princess.

When word came that her barge had entered the Tiber, preparations intensified, and the assembled bands made ready to welcome the Princess. Shortly her barge came in sight, and as it did, there was a tremendous burst of sound as the musicians played for her welcome.

As her barge arrived at the landing dock, the Emperor and Quintus both were standing there waiting to escort Princess Leah to the throne that had been placed next to that of the Emperor on the reviewing stand. When Princess Leah appeared, there was a gasp among all those who were assembled there. Her beauty was striking. And yet, her demeanor was absolutely subdued. She gave no evidence that she felt she was different or more privileged than anyone else.

As she left the barge, she proceeded to the Emperor and went as if to kiss his hand. The Emperor brushed it aside. "Leah, it is I who should be kissing your hand. Has anyone told you how beautiful you are, how striking your appearance?" The Emperor paused and then continued, "Welcome to Rome. All of Rome will now be at your feet my dear Princess. Please come with me to the throne so that we can begin the welcome ceremony."

Claudius escorted Princess Leah to the throne, followed closely by Quintus. There was no throne for Quintus, of course, but there was a place for him to stand beside Princess Leah. Quintus noticed that Leah crossed herself as the ceremony began. He leaned over and whispered, "Are you a Christian?"

Leah looked at him and said very quietly, "Yes, I am. I have been a Christian ever since Peter and Mark visited Egypt and preached about Jesus. I heard him, was convinced, and was baptized on the spot. I have been a devoted and devout Christian ever since."

Looking again directly at Quintus she asked, "Are you a Christian, Quintus?"

Quintus laughed. "No, I am not a Christian, but I may be called a fellow traveler. I believe everything that they say about Jesus and I believe in the concept of Christianity, but I am not a baptized Christian."

Leah looked at him again and added, "I'm looking forward to having some interesting discussions with you. I understand that you are a great friend of Peter and of Paul, and that both have visited you recently. Perhaps they can visit while I am here in Rome. I would greatly like to see Peter again."

Quintus look brightly at Leah and said, "I will arrange it."

With that, the music started, and the welcome ceremony began. It went on for three hours. At the end, Leah graciously took her leave of the Emperor and accompanied Quintus as he directed the litter and the accompanying guards. They proceeded to Quintus' villa which he had prepared for the

Princess. Once they arrived, he gave her time to ready herself for the welcome banquet.

Quintus had arranged for Peter and Paul to attend the banquet. When they arrived and greeted the princess, her glee and happiness could not be contained.

All of the assembled guests were taken with the beauty and poise of Princess Leah. She spoke excellent Latin; little did they know she spoke three other languages as well.

Throughout, Quintus beamed. He was extremely happy to see the Princess again, and he was especially pleased at the regal manner in which she greeted all of his friends whom he had invited to meet her.

The evening wore on with many accolades, many toasts, and much discussion amongst groups of friends. Peter and Paul, in particular, spent a considerable amount of time talking to Princess Leah. Quintus was pleased. He knew that his arrival reception had pleased the Princess, and anything that pleased her pleased him. When the evening ended and the guests gradually left, Peter and Paul were the last to leave. They all had a few minutes together and Princess Leah reminded Peter that he had baptized her after his presentation at the palace of the Pharaoh in Egypt. Peter grinned. "Thank you for the compliment. Let me welcome you again as a fellow Christian."

Shortly after that, Peter and Paul took their leave. At that point, Quintus turned to the Princess and said, "Thank you for coming. I hope you are comfortable here in my villa. I will be next door in the villa of a friend."

With that he took her hand, kissed it, and left.

# CHAPTER NINE

Everywhere Quintus took Leah during her visit, she made an immediate and highly favorable impression. Her bearing, her beauty, and total composure captivated whomever she met. Quintus took her on a tour of all of his friends in Rome and also orchestrated a number of banquets at his villa. All of his friends were captivated by Leah. Many of them came up to Quintus, and with a wink and a nod, encouraged him to pursue her.

When Quintus and Peter had a chance for a private time together, Quintus recalled the conversation with Peter the night of the banquet regarding Leah's conversion to Christianity. Peter said, "She is a godsend. You should ask her opinion as to whether or not she believes in the real presence." Quintus was surprised but agreed to do so. At an opportune moment he did ask Leah if she believed in the real presence. She looked him straight in the eyes and said, "Of course I do." She then went on to say, "I wasn't there at the Seder dinner, but Peter was. I believe Peter. If Peter is convinced, then that is enough for me."

Quintus paused for a moment then rather abruptly said, "But Leah, surely you have your own opinion and do not depend on the beliefs and opinions of others."

Leah laughed. Her laughter was like a tinkering of a musical instrument. "Quintus, I can't believe you are saying that. You know very well that all of us depend upon what other people tell us, and whether or not we accept what they're saying as being true."

Then in a very direct manner stated: "Quintus, you have been in battle. You have survived these battles, and you have comported yourself extremely well in them. But I am certain that you relied heavily upon information which you had received from trusted subordinates or friends or other Tribunes. Is that not so?"

Quintus laughed, "Leah, for someone who has not fought in battles, you understand totally. Battle is nothing but confusion. Victory goes to those who have the best information. In this particular case, I agree with you. It is very important for Christians to understand that Peter believes totally in the transformation of bread and wine into the body and blood of Jesus. You believe it. I think it is true, but I can't quite bring myself to accept it because I do not have the faith that you have. Perhaps the day may come when I do, but at this time, I do not."

Quintus decided to tell Leah what he was doing to satisfy the request of Peter. "I have collected significant studies and research in Rome and Italy outside of the city of Rome. I expect to have this information in the next few weeks. What I report will depend heavily on the findings."

Leah smiled broadly. "Since you have to wait for the results to come, why don't you come to Egypt with me? The trip on the barge will be pleasant and we will have plenty of time to get to know each other more. Besides that, I want you to meet my father." And with that, Leah looked down demurely. The last statement was very important to Quintus because it gave him an indication that she shared a regard for him. He was excited and was pleased that there was some indication that she was as captivated with him as he was with her. He decided to accept her invitation and go with her to Egypt. From there, he could travel to Ephesus where he wanted to meet with John, and once again with Maryam.

Quintus immediately took his leave and proceeded to his meeting room where he had his guard and his villa manager meet with him. He had word sent to John that he wished to see him in Ephesus and hopefully meet with Maryam at the same time. He arranged for a small cohort of legionaries to accompany him on the trip to Egypt. They would mingle with the guards of the Princess

Leah to form a suitable support and protection detail for them. Once they arrived in Egypt, of course, Leah's father would be sure to provide significant protection for them.

Quintus returned to Leah and informed her that he was preparing for the trip. She smiled excitedly and said: "I knew you would do it, Quintus." Then she quietly took his hand and said, "Quintus, you are a better man and a more attractive man than you think you are. You are a great soldier, but you are also a very handsome man."

Quintus was startled as he was taken completely off guard by these comments, but he grinned broadly. He was right. The attraction was mutual.

Quintus took his leave and returned to continue the preparations necessary for his departure for a significant period of time. He also sent word to the Emperor of what he was planning to do, with the request that they meet so that he, Quintus, could be informed of any program that the Emperor wish fulfilled in Egypt. Egypt was an important ally of Rome and had been since the time of Julius Caesar and Mark Anthony. Quintus wanted to make sure that his actions and his words did nothing to disrupt that relationship. Hence, he sought the meeting with the Emperor.

Word came back rather quickly that the Emperor did indeed wish to meet with Quintus. He would receive Quintus upon his arrival at the palace.

Quintus immediately departed for the palace and a few minutes later entered the meeting room. Shortly afterwards, the Emperor appeared and walked directly over to Quintus and took him by the arm. "Quintus, I am captivated by the Princess Leah. I think that your travel and accompanying her to Egypt is a tremendous step forward for you personally. With regard to the affairs of state, I trust you completely in your demeanor and words while you are in Egypt. The fact that Leah is the daughter of the Pharaoh of Egypt is indicative of the levels of conversations that you will have. Go with my fondest regards and hope that your pursuit of the Princess is successful." With that, he smiled broadly, slapped Quintus on the shoulder, and took his leave.

Quintus was pleased. He knew that he was accepted by the Emperor and considered one of his favorites. With this enthusiasm for Princess Leah and his absolute enthusiasm of hearing of Quintus' proposed trip to Egypt, the Emperor was very pleased. Quintus left in a very happy mood and returned to his villa looking forward to when he would be with Leah again that day.

## CHAPTER TEN

Quintus knew that for the first time in his life he had met someone that he wanted to share his life with. He was certain that Leah had the same desire.

With the blessing of the Emperor for their trip to Egypt they embarked on the barge. Quintus and Leah were accompanied by a cohort of legionaries to protect them at all times.

The trip was uneventful. It provided a great deal of time for Leah and Quintus to talk. During one particularly brilliant moonlit night as they sat on the deck of the barge, Leah said to Quintus, "I've always loved you. From the time I was a little girl and saw you as a solider in Egypt, I became enchanted with your manliness and your bearing, and hoped that someday you would return that love."

Quintus was startled. Everything he had hoped for he finally realized was true. He very quietly took Leah's hand and said, "Leah you must know that I care greatly for you. I am coming because I want to discuss with your father the possibility of you becoming my bride."

Leah smiled and leaned over and kissed Quintus. "Quintus you have made me unbelievably happy. I wish to be your wife. We will see what my

73

father has to say, but I am sure that I will be able to persuade him."

Quintus smiled, "I am sure you will."

The next day they entered the Nile and proceeded to the docking area at the capital, Cairo. By mid-afternoon they had docked. They left the barge and were proceeding to the Pharaoh's palace. Pharaoh had sent an escort to the barge to meet them.

When they arrived at the Pharaoh's palace, the Pharaoh was there to greet them. He immediately embraced Leah and then turned to Quintus, "Welcome to our land. Your fame has preceded you. Thank you for accompanying my daughter back to Egypt. I wish to discuss a few matters with you." With that he took Quintus by the arm and led him into the palace to a meeting room. After they were seated and had been served refreshments, Pharaoh turned to Quintus, and said very casually and politely, "What are your intentions concerning my daughter?" The Pharaoh sounded like a real father and not the Pharaoh of Egypt.

Quintus began, "Pharaoh, your daughter and I have fallen in love. We seek to be married. Do I have your permission to do so?"

The Pharaoh smiled. This came as no surprise to him. But he felt it necessary to raise some very delicate points with Quintus. "Quintus, you must imagine the expense of keeping someone like Leah in her usual style of living. Do you have the means to do so?"

Quintus paused for a few moments before answering, "Pharaoh, I have more than sufficient means to keep her in the lifestyle of life in Rome. I do not know if those means are sufficient for her style of life in Egypt. I need some guidance on that."

The Pharaoh laughed, "I can arrange that very quickly by granting you lands and the wherewithal to provide her with her normal standard of life here in Egypt. I would assume that you two will live in Egypt and in Rome. I am satisfied that you will be able to take care of her in Rome. Hence, I leave it to the two of you to decide if and when you wish to wed. Please let me know so that I can make the appropriate arrangements here if you decide to have the wedding in Egypt, which I hope you will do."

After a very short pause, Quintus said, "Pharaoh, there is no doubt that the ceremony will be here in Egypt, but I will confirm this with Leah."

The Pharaoh and Quintus exited from the meeting room and sought out Princess Leah. When they were together, the Pharaoh said, "My dear Leah, I have given permission for you two to wed. Please let me know the date that you select for this so I can make the appropriate arrangement for this to be the royal wedding it truly is."

Leah smiled graciously and then abruptly stopped and demurely looked down. "Thank you, father. Yes, I do want the wedding to be here in Egypt and I would ask that you pick the appropriate time so that you have the ability to make all the necessary arrangements."

Quintus said: "Thank you Leah and thank you Pharaoh. While these preparations are being made, I will travel to Ephesus since I wish to discuss certain matters with John who is there. By the time I return, I am sure that all of your arrangements will be made."

"That is an excellent idea, Quintus," quipped the Pharaoh. To be honest with you, the groom is somewhat of an annoyance while preparations for a wedding go on. You must know that all brides make all the choices, even though the father of the bride is supposedly that one in charge. Do you wish to travel over land or by sea?"

Quintus answered, "Whichever is faster. I believe it would be best to go by sea, but I prefer a fast galleon as opposed to a comfortable barge."

The Pharaoh smiled. "Quintus, you are satisfying my concept of your reputation as being a man of action. I will see that the galleon is made ready for you tomorrow. It has been a pleasure meeting you and I look forward to spending significant time with you in the future."

After a short pause the Pharaoh looked directly at Quintus, "Welcome to the family. Please take care of my daughter, I love her greatly." And with that the Pharaoh bowed and took his leave.

Quintus and Leah continued to discuss many things for the rest of the day. The next day, Quintus returned to the docking area and saw a fast galleon ready for him. His contingent of the Praetorian Guard came aboard and shortly thereafter they left for Ephesus.

## CHAPTER ELEVEN

The trip to Ephesus was uneventful, although tedious in its length. But ultimately, they did arrive at the port Ephesus. Upon docking, there was a short overland journey to Ephesus, Quintus asked for John. He was told that John had gone to the island of Patmos, but that he had built a home for Maryam. Quintus asked for directions and proceeded to the house.

As he approached her home, Maryam came out to greet Quintus. She smiled and said, "Quintus, how good it is to see you again. Welcome to my humble home. I know that you wish to see John, and that he is now in Patmos, to which you can travel tomorrow. For now, come in and talk to me."

Quintus was surprised. How did she know he was coming? How did she still remember his name? He remembered his meeting with her in Judea where he had felt surrounded by her love. Once again, he felt surrounded by a curtain of love.

He followed her into her sitting room and they quietly sat and talked.

"Quintus, I knew you were coming. I knew you would be here today. I know what you wish to discuss with me. Very briefly, let me tell you that

Jesus loved beyond all measure. I cannot tell you how deep that love was. He loved everyone. He hoped only that the love would be reciprocated and that everyone would live a life without evil. That is why He instituted the rite of changing bread and wine into His body and blood. It was not just to provide a remembrance of Him, but also to provide an aid to all those who participate in leading a good life. That was his final act of love. And now, Quintus, what else can I tell you?"

Quintus was surprised, but then again, he wasn't. Maryam was the mother of Jesus, the mother of God, and of course he would leave her with special talents and special capabilities. The fact that she knew of his mission before he arrived was significant to him. What was even more significant, was how quickly and succinctly she confirmed everything that he had heard from many people concerning the rite of changing bread and wine into the body and blood of Jesus.

"Maryam, I cannot tell you how grateful I am for your receiving me, spending time with me, and providing me with information that will be vital for me in arriving at a decision as to how to prove unequivocally that bread and wine are changed into the body and blood of Jesus; for this is the real presence. Your words will go a long way toward providing me with the logic and facts to prove that the real presence is true."

They continued to talk for a while, reminiscing about Judea and about Jesus. Throughout Quintus continued to feel this surrounding blanket of love and comfort. After a short time, he took his leave, and proceeded back to the dock area where he boarded the galleon and left immediately for Patmos. He arrived later that day and upon disembarking, sought out John. He found him and made him aware of why he had come to meet with him.

John laughed. "You've come all this way to ask my opinion as to the real presence of Jesus and the changed bread and wine." John laughed again. "Of course, Jesus is present. The bread and wine are changed into his body and blood. This is so. I was there when he initiated the rite, and I have performed the rite myself many times, and as Jesus directed, I have anointed others who also perform the rite. Quintus, you can be assured that as a direct witness at the Seder dinner, the bread and wine are changed into the body and blood of Jesus."

John paused for a moment and then looked very meaningfully at Quintus, "Quintus, do you have any doubts? I know there are those who will claim this is a symbolic act rather than a real act, but that is not true. Jesus said, 'Do this in memory of me', meaning the changing of bread and wine into his body and blood. He did not say do this as the symbolism of that act but do it as a direct act. There is no doubt whatsoever as to what he meant and what he said."

John then went on to explain that Jesus, in response to the Pharisees' question "Who do you think you are?" said, "Your father Abraham rejoiced at the thought of seeing my day; he saw it and was glad." "You are not yet fifty years old," the Jews said to him, "and you have seen Abraham!" "I tell you the truth," Jesus answered, "before Abraham was, I AM!" At this, they picked up stones to stone him, but Jesus hid himself, slipping away from the temple grounds. The violent response of the Jews to Jesus' "I AM" statement indicates they clearly understood what He was declaring — that He was the eternal God incarnate. Jesus was equating Himself with the "I AM" title God gave Himself.

Quintus had listened very carefully to John. He had come a long way to hear these words, and he did not take them lightly. He knew they were the absolute truth. And so, he very quietly said, "Thank you, John. You have confirmed what I have heard from Peter, Paul, others, Maryam, and now yourself. Thank you. I will be in a very strong position to prepare my report."

"Well Quintus, how many thousand people do you have to have say the same thing before you believe it? Isn't it enough that Peter, Paul and I have said the same thing?"

"I have no reservations at all. It is merely a piece of wanting to be complete so that my report will leave no doubt whatsoever on this question. I must satisfy the unbelievers by raising the issue as to how they can doubt what they have seen with their own eyes and heard with their own ears. I am sure that none of those who saw Jesus do this at the Seder dinner will have any doubts. It is those who were not present who may have doubts and to whom it is necessary for me to provide sufficient evidence to convince them. That is why I am seeking so many opinions and listening very carefully."

John laughed. "Good luck, Quintus. I don't envy your task at dealing with the naysayers. Throughout history, they have been consistent at denying what they have seen with their own eyes, heard with their own ears, or have been told by trustworthy people."

The two continued to talk for a short period of time and then Quintus took his leave and proceeded back to the galleon and embarked on the return trip to Egypt. He was satisfied that he now had incontrovertible evidence from Peter and Paul and Maryam that Jesus did indeed institute the rite of changing bread and wine into His body and blood. Quintus was equally sure that he still had to convince the naysayers. But the more evidence he had, the stronger his ability to change their opinions.

As he looked out to sea, he thought of Leah and the wedding that would occur upon his arrival back in Egypt.

## CHAPTER TWELVE

When Quintus returned to Cairo, he found that the palace and indeed the entire city, was bustling with preparation for the wedding. He knew it was an important element in his life, but he did not know the extent to which it became a national event for Princess Leah. Of course, it should be. She was the daughter of the Pharaoh. Her marriage was indeed a state ceremony.

Quintus decided to make himself available if needed but to remain mostly in the background so as not to create any disruption to the preparations as they went on. He listened very carefully to the instructions given to him by the director of the wedding as to what he should do, where he should be, and even to the extent of suggesting what he might say at all times. The marriage vows were certainly fixed but everything else was variable. This was to be a Christian wedding, even if it was being conducted in a pagan temple. Peter had been asked to come to consecrate the marriage. He came with Mark and spent some time with Quintus before the wedding.

Quintus was surprised when Peter asked him if he was sorry for all of his sins. Quintus said, "I am not aware of any sins that I committed but I am sorry for all of them."

Peter laughed. He then said to Quintus, "By the power given to me I forgive you your sins."

Quintus looked directly at Peter and said, "Is this something else that Jesus gave you at the Seder dinner?"

"Yes. He not only gave us the power to change bread and wine into his body and blood, but he also gave us the power to forgive sins. As he said it, 'Those sins you shall forgive are forgiven and those sins you shall retain are retained.'"

Quintus said, "I can see where Jesus instituted a form of priesthood at that dinner."

"Yes, he did!" said Peter.

When the preparations were complete, Quintus was told the marriage ceremony would take place the next day. He spent the evening with Peter in quiet contemplation. Peter led him in a series of specific points. Quintus soon realized that Peter was leading him in prayer. He found the effort invigorating.

The next day, Quintus and his troop proceeded to the pagan temple that had been prepared for the Christian wedding.

Just before the wedding ceremony, Quintus had an opportunity to meet quietly with Peter. With conviction he stated, "Peter, I can prove that the presence is real, that bread and wine are changed into the body and blood of Jesus at all times in the consecration of the 'misa'."

Peter looks up in surprise. "You know, Quintus, I never doubted that for a second. I asked you to look into it so we could put aside the doubts of people with little faith or understanding. What did you find?"

Quintus chuckled. "Peter, you know very well that what you asked me to do was the truth, cut and dried. Jesus did make those statements, and he did have the power and authority to make it happen. Simple statements such as that to John, 'Before Abraham was, I AM' is prima fascia evidence that Jesus claims to be God, has demonstrated such power on more than one occasion, and certainly had the power to change bread and wine into His body and blood."

Quintus chuckled again, "And there's your proof, period. Now let's go get me married."

Peter stood at the front of the temple, and Quintus stood to the side. At a given moment, Princess Leah, preceded by her attendants, began walking down the aisle on the arm of her father, the

Pharaoh. Music was playing as she approached Quintus. Coming to him, she bowed to Peter and left the arm of her father who had accompanied her down the aisle and together with Quintus, stood before Peter as he read the marriage vows. As the ceremony continued, Peter turned and began praying and said the magic words, "I pronounce you man and wife."

At the appropriate moment, he presented Leah with bread and a cup. Leah ate the bread and then drank from the cup. He did not present it to Quintus.

Following this, Quintus and Leah proceeded down the aisle and exited from the temple. Surrounded by their guards, they were escorted to the Pharaoh's palace for the reception.

A great room had been highly decorated. Leah and Quintus greeted individually the guests as they came. The guests included Claudius and his wife, Agrippina. They were accompanied by Nero, the son of Agrippina. Other dignitaries were Paul, John, and the head of the Praetorian guards.

As each distinguished guest came, Leah and Quintus had some words with them.

For the Emperor Claudius and his wife, Agrippina, Quintus was very gracious, thanking the Emperor for making the trip to Cairo for his wedding. He was surprised that Agrippina seemed cold. He went so far as to ask her if she were enjoying the wedding. She smiled playfully and said nothing but introduced her son, Nero. She introduced him as the next Emperor of Rome. Nero was sullen but was gracious enough to offer his congratulations to the bride and groom. He then turned to Quintus, and said casually but meaningfully, "You had better behave yourself, Senator, when I am Emperor. I will not tolerate much of the nonsense that you seem to be engaged in continually."

Quintus was taken aback and somewhat surprised. He did not know the source of this malcontent statement from Nero, but he surmised that it was the doing of Agrippina and partly the vicious nature of Nero. He said rather evenly to Nero, "Remember Nero, that I am a person of power within the Empire. I also have the Equestrian guard behind me at all times. I would suggest that you make no effort to constrain me in any way. I hope you understand that."

Nero was surprised at the forcefulness of Quintus. Agrippina stepped in at this time and glossed over the situation with meaningless words that confused the pending disagreement. When Nero, Agrippina, and Claudius had moved away, Leah asked Quintus what that was all about.

Looking at her he said, "I really do not know. I never did anything to offend Nero even though I have nothing but contempt for that evil man. God help him if he tries to exert a kind of difficulty so consistent with his nature. I see great troubles for Rome if he ever becomes Emperor."

Leah asked, "Is there no alternative?"

Quintus wishfully said, "I wish there were. I don't think so. Agrippina is determined to place Nero on the throne. We only hope that she will allow nature to take its course, rather than precipitate an early death for Claudius. She is notorious for feeding her husband poison mushrooms. I told Claudius to make sure he didn't eat any mushrooms presented to him by Agrippina."

Leah laughed, "If it wasn't so tragic, it would be funny."

"It is not so funny if you are fed poison mushrooms by your wife," said Quintus. "But then again Agrippina may be his official wife, but she is certainly no wife to Claudius."

The reception continued. Quintus and Leah left for a honeymoon on the Nile River. They were accompanied by a significant cohort of the Equestrian guard.

## CHAPTER THIRTEEN

After the honeymoon the couple returned to Cairo. Shortly thereafter they returned to Rome. In their absence Quintus' villa had been prepared for their life there. To say the least, it had progressed from elegant to sumptuous. Leah was pleased.

Quintus retired to his study and sat quietly, a piece of papyrus before him. He very carefully thought out the entire circumstances surrounding the declaration by Jesus at the Seder dinner the night before he died that: "This is my body…" And so, Quintus began to write.

Jesus was not given to hyperbole. He had a track record and a history of miracles. He changed water into wine at the wedding feast of Cana. He fed thousands of disciples with seven loaves and two fishes. When His feeding of them was complete, twelve baskets of crumbs were assembled. Jesus raised three people or more from the dead. Three at least that could be verified by name. He Himself, raised Himself from the dead. These are not minor accomplishments of someone without superpower. Hence, He certainly had the power to change bread into His body and wine into His blood.

Did He?

Once again, Jesus was not given to hyperbole. There are no instances anywhere in any of the written recordings of His life, which indicate that Jesus made outrageous comments as an attention grabber or as something He used to get the attentions of His followers. Hence it can be assumed that He really believed that He was about to change the bread into His body, and the wine into His blood as He said He would. Then He did it!

The final part of His saying is "Do this as a commemoration of me." There are some who would claim that what He meant was to have a simulation of that conversion done. This is very unlikely. Once again, Jesus was not given to hyperbole. When He said, "Do this…," He meant to do the conversion of bread and wine into His body and blood.

That was the request of Jesus. He was not asking that there be a show of that as a performance. He assumed He was asking His followers to do just that as the real thing.

In addition, during the Seder dinner, He did institute and give to His followers, the power to forgive sins, and to retain sins. This power is significant.

What Jesus was doing during the Seder dinner was establishing, a priesthood of the anointed ones, and secondly, a set of ceremonials associated with His life and persona. The most important of these was the power to change bread and wine into His body and blood.

Finally, throughout His period of teaching, Jesus did all He could to train and convince His followers that they had the power to do what He was transmitting to them. There was no doubt that what He intended was to establish not only a priesthood, but a set of sacraments that would provide signs that He was always accompanying His followers. Hence, the consecration of bread and wine into His body and blood would then produce a sacrament which could be distributed to the people to enhance their spirit, and their faith in Jesus.

The universal charity of Jesus was shown by His words "which is given to you" and "which is poured out for you." This was a gift of Jesus to His followers. It was a gift to encourage their faith, and to be a remembrance of all times of His sacrifice, His passion, and death. The consecration of bread and wine into His body and blood is real. It is the perpetuation of His gift to His beloved people.

Consider now, the alternative. That Jesus did not have the power to change bread and wine into His body and blood. There is no evidence of this. In fact, on the contrary, there is significant evidence that He certainly did have the power. Second, consider that Jesus did not mean to actually change bread and wine into His body and blood. If that were so, why did He say He was doing it? There is no history of Jesus saying things He did not mean.

Third point, that Jesus meant that there is only to be a simulation of this and not a true conversion. This is not what He said. And when He provided the power to His followers with the words, "Do this…", then there is no doubt that the real presence always occurs when His anointed ones say the words, "This is my body…"

Having summarized the situation in this fashion, Quintus then turned to the testimony of various people with whom he spoke.

First of all, all of the Apostles who attended the Seder dinner, did indeed verify that Jesus did change bread and wine into His body and blood. They also verified that He asked them to continue to do that in remembrance of Him, and in order to provide support for those who became His followers. The support would be by the consummation of His body and blood following the consecration that changed bread and wine as such into His body and blood.

Quintus could find no credible person who denied this conversion. He did find evidence that there were some Christians who did not believe that this was indeed the body and blood of Jesus Christ. On the other hand, he found a significant percentage of those interviewed who did so believe.

Quintus was convinced that those who had doubts and did not believe could be converted to a full belief if all of the facts were pointed out to them, and if they had an opportunity to discuss the matter with believers.

Taking all of this into account, Quintus concluded that the process of consecration and conversion was real: that Jesus did change bread and wine into His body and blood; and that anointed ones did continue to change bread and wine into His body and blood.

Quintus sat there and quietly observed that in centuries to come, this controversy would continue. But there would remain no doubt whatsoever on the part of a significant number of Christians that indeed the consecration process did change bread and wine into the body and blood of Jesus.

All of this was in the future. For the present, however, the consecration process did produce the real presence of Jesus Christ.

Quintus was prepared to make his report to Peter. He knew that this would be no surprise to Peter, but he knew that Peter would be gratified that an impartial examiner and observer such as Quintus would conclude that the real presence did exist.

Quintus sat quietly for a few moments. Was he becoming a Christian? Quintus still felt that he did not have the faith to accept what he believed. That was the difference between him and a Christian. A Christian had the faith to accept even when they could not understand how it could happen. He did not understand how it could happen, he firmly believed it did happen, but he did not have the faith to bridge the gap. Perhaps the day would come when he would become a Christian.

## CHAPTER FOURTEEN

Some months later, Leah was pregnant. The birth was difficult one and like a typical father, Quintus paced up and down until he heard the cry of the baby. He immediately fell in love with the baby, a boy. He would be named Septimus Gaius Caesar.

The first few days after his birth were difficult. Then the baby developed a raging fever. The doctor sent by the Pharaoh said that the baby would die. Quintus refused to accept this. He called Mark, who came and blessed the baby, and turned to Quintus and said, "Let us pray." He fell on his knees and Quintus did the same. As Mark prayed to Jesus, and to the Holy Spirit, and to God the Father, Quintus echoed his words. Then he added his own. "He is such an innocent little baby. Please, please, please, do not let him die."

They rose together and went over to the baby. Mark put his hands on the baby's brow and made the sign of the cross. The baby let out a gurgle. Quintus touched the baby and found that the fever had gone. Quintus turned to Mark, "Your prayers are effective, Mark," he said.

Mark smiled and calmly added: "Not only my prayers but yours, Quintus. This is what it is all about. We've been told repeatedly by Jesus to ask

97

and it will be given to us. We asked, and it was given to us. Always remember, Jesus is there, ready to help us at all time. Try it, Quintus. If you are in difficulty, do not forget to pray."

Mark left. All this time, Leah had been sitting in the back of the room watching and praying. When it was reported that the baby's fever had disappeared, she gave a sigh and a beatific smile came over her face. She turned to Quintus and said, "Quintus, by this time you must believe. You have not only all the evidence of all of your investigations, but you now have your own son cured from a disease that many of the doctors, my father sent, said would be fatal. I did not believe them. I truly believed that God would intervene and save our baby. Quintus, do you not believe?"

Quintus did not answer but kneeled and put his hands together, raised them on high and said, "Thank you, Lord." As he did so, his whole body was engulfed in a blanket of peace. He bowed his head and said, "My Lord and my God."